T0142650

Arthur

Saves the Day

Author: Walter C Kilgus

Illustrator: Craig Howarth

Copyright © 2021 by Walter C Kilgus. 811582

All rights reserved. No part of this book may
be reproduced or transmitted in any form or by
any means, electronic or mechanical, including
photocopying, recording, or by any information
storage and retrieval system, without permission in
writing from the copyright owner.

This is a work of fiction. Names, characters,
places and incidents either are the product of the
author's imagination or are used fictitiously, and
any resemblance to any actual persons, living or
dead, events, or locales is entirely coincidental.

To order additional copies of this book, contact:
Xlibris
844-714-8691
www.Xlibris.com
Orders@Xlibris.com

ISBN: Softcover   978-1-6641-4975-5
       Hardcover   978-1-6641-4976-2
       EBook   978-1-6641-4974-8

Print information available on the last page

Rev. date: 01/06/2021

LITTLE BEULAH BEAR SAID TO HERSELF, "I'D LIKE SOME HONEY TODAY, AS SHE WENT ALONG THE PATH BY THE ROCK CREEK ON A FINE SUMMER DAY."

SHE SPIED A BEEHIVE UP IN A TREE, AND THOUGHT, "I'LL BET HONEY'S UP THERE JUST WAITING FOR ME."

SHE CLIMBED UP THE TREE AND OUT ON THE LIMB, CHANCES
OF REACHING THE HIVE WERE REALLY QUITE SLIM.

JUST AS SHE REACHED FOR THE HONEY IN THE HIVE, THE TREE LIMB BROKE AND BEULAH BEGAN A TERRIBLE DIVE DOWN TOWARD THE RUSHING ROCK CREEK, WHERE SHE MIGHT NOT SURVIVE.

BEULAH LANDED ON A LEDGE HALFWAY UP, HALFWAY DOWN. IF SHE FELL ANY FURTHER, SHE WAS SURE SHE WOULD DROWN.

AS ALWAYS, WHEN IN TROUBLE BEULAH STARTED TO CRY AND THE SOUND OF HER SOBBING DRIFTED UP TO THE SKY.

ARTHUR AND GRANDMA'S SHEEPDOG CHAUCER WERE IN THE WOODS THAT DAY TOO. JUST WANDERING AROUND WITHOUT MUCH TO DO.

THEY HEARD SOBBING AND CRYING DOWN BY THE CREEK, SO THEY WENT TO THE EDGE OF THE CLIFF AND TOOK A QUICK PEEK.

THERE THEY SAW BEULAH STRANDED BELOW, BUT HOW THEY COULD HELP HER; THEY REALLY DIDN'T KNOW.

ARTHUR SAID TO CHAUCER, "I'LL GO BACK TO THE HOUSE
AND GET GRANDPA'S OLD CLIMBING ROPE. YOU GO GET
THE OTHER ANIMALS, IT'S BEULAH'S ONLY HOPE,"

ARTHUR RAN BACK TO THE HOUSE, GRANDPA'S ROPE HE
WAS HOPING TO FIND.

CHAUCER RACED THROUGH THE WOODS CALLING TO
THE ANIMALS OF EVERY SHAPE AND KIND.

THE ANIMALS CAME TO THE EDGE OF THE CLIFF IN ONES
AND IN TWOS AND BEGAN TO TALK ABOUT JUST WHAT
THEY COULD DO.

ARTHUR RAN UP AND SAID, "I HAVE A PLAN AND I THINK WE SHOULD TRY IT AS FAST AS WE CAN. FIRST, WE WILL TIE THE ROPE AROUND ME, THEN LOWER ME OVER THE EDGE, DO IT VERY CAREFULLY!"

SO, ARTHUR VERY BRAVELY STEPPED OVER THE EDGE.
THE ANIMALS HELD ON TIGHTLY AS THEY LOWERED HIM
DOWN TO THE LEDGE.

ARTHUR SAID TO BEULAH, "I'LL SEND YOU UP ON THE ROPE. THEN THE ANIMALS WILL PULL ME UP AND THIS WILL BE OVER I HOPE."

BEULAH SAID, "I WON'T KNOW WHAT TO DO UNLESS I GO UP WHILE HOLDING ON TO YOU." SO, ARTHUR TIED THE ROPE AROUND BOTH OF THEM TIGHT. HE CALLED TO THE ANIMALS AND SAID, "PULL WITH ALL OF YOUR MIGHT!"

SO, THE ANIMALS PULLED AND THEY PULLED, BUT THEY
COULDN'T BRING THEM UP. THEIR MUSCLES GOT SORE
AND THEY THOUGHT THEY WOULD HAVE TO GIVE UP.

BUT FELIX FOX SHOUTED TO OLIVIA OWL, "WE NEED JUST ONE MORE, SEE IF YOU CAN FIND WILLIE, THE WILD BOAR."

SO, OLIVIA FLEW OFF AND FOUND WILLIE ASLEEP.

SHE SHOUTED, "WILLIE, COME WITH ME TO THE LEDGE
AT THE ROCK CREEK."

WHEN WILLIE ARRIVED, HE TOOK HOLD OF THE END OF THE ROPE.

THE ANIMALS PULLED AGAIN, BUT NOW THEY HAD HOPE.

THEY PULLED AND THEY PULLED AND DIDN'T STOP UNTIL
ARTHUR AND BEULAH POPPED OVER THE TOP.

THE ANIMALS WERE EXHAUSTED, BUT FULL OF GOOD CHEER. THEY SAID, "WE'RE SURE GLAD THAT ARTHUR WAS HERE."

ARTHUR SAID, "THE PLAN TO RESCUE BEULAH TURNED OUT TO BE GOOD, AND EVERYONE HELPED AS MUCH AS THEY COULD."

SO, ARTHUR TOOK THE ROPE AND WENT BACK THROUGH THE WOODS AND CAME TO THE HOUSE WHERE GRANDPA STOOD.

GRANDPA SAID, "ARTHUR, WHAT ARE YOU DOING WITH MY ROPE?" ARTHUR SAID, "WE USED IT TO SAVE BEULAH. THAT WAS OK I HOPE?" THEN ARTHUR TOLD GRANDPA WHAT HAD HAPPENED THAT DAY.

GRANDPA SAID, "ARTHUR, THAT WAS A BRAVE THING TO DO. IT WAS GOOD THAT YOU WERE ABLE TO COME TO BEULAH'S RESCUE."

THE END

Printed in the United States
By Bookmasters